Cinderella

Beauty AND THE BEAST

A Movie Theater Storybook

Adapted by Rita Balducci

Illustrated by the Disney Storybook Artists

CONTENTS

Reader's Digest Children's Books®

Pleasantville, New York • Montréal, Québec • Bath, United Kingdom

Cinderella

*O*nce upon a time, there was a lovely young girl who lived with her widowed father.

DISK 1

1 She was happy and kind to all. However, her father felt that she needed a mother, and in time he married a woman with two

2 young daughters of her own.

When her dear father died, the young girl soon learned the true natures of her cruel stepmother and stepsisters. They called her Cinderella and

3 forced her to do all the work of the household. She sang as she cooked and cleaned and never complained about her

hard life. Cinderella dreamed that
someday the wishes dear to her heart
would come true, and she would find
true love and happiness. The barnyard
animals became her
companions, and
she was so gentle
that even the birds
and mice did not
fear her.

4 Gus and Jaq were two mice that Cinderella fed and dressed. They loved her dearly and wished they could do something to help her.

One day, an invitation arrived from the royal palace. "There's to be a ball," the stepmother read. "Every eligible maiden is to attend."

"Why, I can go, too!" Cinderella cried.

5 Her stepmother agreed, *if* Cinderella managed to finish her work. Gus and Jaq and

6 the other mice and birds decided to surprise Cinderella. They sewed a lovely gown while she worked at her chores.

Cinderella was overjoyed to find the beautiful dress in her attic room. She put it on and rushed to join her stepsisters.

7 "Look! That's my sash!" cried one in a jealous rage.

"Those are my beads!" shrieked the other. They tore at Cinderella's dress until it was tattered and ruined. Poor

8 Cinderella ran to the garden in despair.

As she wept, Cinderella became aware of a gentle hand stroking her hair and a soft voice speaking to her.

"Who are you?" Cinderella asked the kindly woman.

"Why, I'm your fairy godmother, child," the woman said. "I've come to help you get to the ball." Then, with a wave of her wand, the mice changed into horses and a pumpkin became a glittering coach.

DISK 2

9

Cinderella was speechless. With another wave of her wand, the Fairy Godmother changed Cinderella's raggedy dress to a beautiful, shimmering gown. Cinderella looked down—she was even wearing sparkling glass slippers!

10

"You must leave the ball before midnight," the fairy godmother told her, "for then the spell will be broken."

As soon as Cinderella entered the ball, the Prince could not take his eyes off her. They danced under the light of the moon, and before long, they had fallen in love.

11   Suddenly, a chime sounded from high above. The clock had begun to strike the midnight hour. "I must go!" Cinderella cried as she ran from the ballroom. In her hurry, one glass shoe slipped from her foot.

12   The Prince picked up the delicate slipper. "I will marry the maiden whose foot fits this slipper," he declared.

The Grand Duke and his footman set out at dawn to find the owner of the glass slipper. In time, they came to Cinderella's house and were relieved to see that the slipper fit neither of the unpleasant stepsisters.

13

What the Grand Duke did not know was that Cinderella had been locked away in the attic by her evil stepmother. Gus and Jaq bravely stole the key and slid it under the door to free Cinderella just in time.

14

Just as the Grand Duke and his footman were preparing to leave with the slipper, Cinderella called to him. "Your Grace! Please wait. May I try it on?"

The wicked stepmother sneered, but there was nothing she could do. Or was

there? Just as the footman passed her, she tripped him with her cane. The glass slipper flew from his hands and shattered at Cinderella's feet.

The Grand Duke gasped in dismay. Just then, Cinderella spoke, "But you see, I have the other slipper." She held out the matching shoe to the delight of the Grand Duke and the horror of her stepmother. It fit her foot perfectly!

Cinderella's dreams had come true! The Prince and Cinderella were married right away, and they lived happily ever after.

Beauty and the Beast

DISK I

1

2

3

*I*n a small town in France, a long time ago, there lived a girl named Belle. She was smart and kind, and she dreamed of leaving her small town to have adventures like the ones she read about in books. Gaston, a vain hunter, hoped to make Belle his wife, but she was not the least bit interested in marrying him.

Belle was quite devoted to her father, an absent-minded inventor. He understood Belle's dreams and wishes, and he loved her more than anything else in the world.

One evening, Belle's father became lost in the woods. He came upon an enormous castle and entered it. To his surprise, he found that the furniture inside

was enchanted. He
was even more
astonished when
a candlestick
named Lumiere
and a clock named
Cogsworth greeted
him and welcomed
him to the castle.

Suddenly, he
heard a fierce growl, and an enormous
beast appeared and cornered him.
"Please, I mean no harm!" Belle's father
begged, but the Beast took him prisoner.

4

When her father didn't come home, Belle set out to search the forest where he had gone. In time, she too came to the Beast's enchanted castle. She found her father locked in a dungeon in the castle.

"You must go right now!" her father warned. But Belle would not leave and she begged the Beast to let her take her father's place as prisoner. The Beast agreed. There was a spell over the castle, and the Beast knew that if Belle came to love him, the spell would be broken. Then he and the enchanted furniture would return to their original human forms.

Belle missed her father terribly, but she
also found the castle to be a strange and

6

wonderful place. The Beast told her she was
free to wander throughout the castle, except
for one room which she was forbidden to
enter. One day, Belle's curiosity got the
better of her and she decided to sneak into
the forbidden room. Inside, she found a

7

rose under a bell jar, glittering and magical.

Just then the Beast bounded into the
room. He was furious that Belle had
disobeyed him. "What are you doing here?"
he shouted angrily. Belle was terrified. She
had never seen the Beast this angry.

Belle fled the castle and ran into the forest. A pack of hungry wolves chased her through the snow. As they were about to attack, the Beast appeared and chased them off, saving Belle's life.

DISK 2

Belle began to look at the Beast differently after he saved her. Soon they became good friends. Lumiere, Cogsworth, and the rest of their castle friends were very excited to see the change in the Beast. It seemed as though the spell was finally going to be broken!

One evening, the Beast decided to tell Belle that he loved her. They shared a romantic evening of dancing under the stars. "Are you happy, Belle?" he gently asked her. Belle told the Beast that she

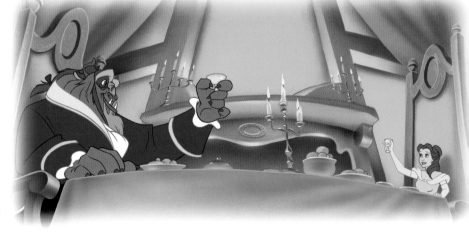

would be happy if she could just see her
father again.

    With a heavy heart, the Beast said,
"You are no longer my prisoner. Take this
magical mirror to remember me."

    Belle's father was overjoyed to see his
daughter again. She told him how the
Beast had changed, and of the many kind
things he had done for her. A knock at the
door interrupted them.

It was Gaston and a crowd of villagers. Belle's father had been telling tales about a strange beast, but no one had believed him. They all thought he was crazy and had come to take him to the insane asylum!

"I can help you and your father, Belle," Gaston said. "*If* you agree to marry me."

"Never!" cried Belle.

Gaston picked up the magical mirror and he saw a reflection of the Beast. "So this is who you care for?" he sneered. He turned to the villagers and shouted, "We must kill this wicked beast!" The angry villagers followed Gaston into the forest, determined to kill the Beast.

12

13 Gaston soon found the Beast in the forbidden tower room. They fought on the slippery castle rooftop. Gaston drew a knife and stabbed the Beast. Suddenly,
14 Gaston lost his footing and fell.

"Beast!" Belle cried, rushing to where he lay wounded. Tears fell from her eyes as she leaned forward, whispering, "I love you."

Slowly, the Beast rose into the air and
15 began to change. Belle watched in astonishment as brilliant beams of light began to dance around him. As his cloak twisted and spun, the Beast was transformed into a handsome young man.

"Belle," he said, holding his hand out to her. Belle looked deeply into the young man's blue eyes. She suddenly realized that the handsome young man and the Beast were one and the same. "It's you!" she cried happily.

As the Beast was transformed, so were the rest of the people from his castle. Soon afterward, they all celebrated the wedding of Beauty and the Beast, and everyone lived happily ever after.

16